ALEX CAGE
CLEAN FAST-PACED ACTION THRILLERS

JOIN THE READER'S LIST

Get the latest releases and exclusive giveaways - sign up to the Alex Cage Reader List:

www.AlexCage.com/signup

ALSO BY ALEX CAGE

Orlando Black Series

Carolina Dance

Bayside Boom

Bet on Black

Leroy Silver Series

Contracts & Bullets

Aloha & Bullets

Politics Thieves & Bullets

Get the latest releases and exclusive giveaways, sign up to the Alex Cage Reader List.

www.AlexCage.com/signup

A DEADLY CHANCE

A CHANCE FREEMAN THRILLER

ALEX CAGE

Copyright Page

This book is a work of fiction. The characters, places, and situations were all created from the author's imagination or used in a fictitious manner and are not to be interpreted as real. Any parallels to actual people, places, or situations, living or dead, is completely unintentional.

A DEADLY CHANCE

1

The first time I saw her, I was sitting at a bar top, ordering hot wings, crinkle cut fries, and a club soda with grapefruit juice. The jazz club's door opened, and she floated across the floor toward me. Sounds from the saxophone, guitar, and piano all dampened as she approached. It was hard to take my eyes away from her. She wore a v-neck, navy-colored wrap midi dress with a slit. Sparkles emitted from her wrist as light struck her diamond-speckled gold bracelet. I glanced away briefly, but my eyes quickly returned to her alluring strides. We fixed on each other when she reached the empty bar. Her baby brown eyes complemented her mocha skin. She sucked in her lips and smoothed her dress before sitting one stool away from me.

"What can I get you, ma'am?" Robby, the bartender, asked.

"For now, I'll just have a Coke," the woman said in a gentle tone which kept the words lingering for seconds after she spoke them.

"You got it," Robby said before turning away.

He glanced at me while shrugging his lips and nodding.

It was a gesture he and I used for years to suggest the appreciation we had for a female's appearance. The woman's shoulder-length, curly, natural hair bounced as she adjusted herself on the stool. She brushed a bundle of curls behind her ear, exposing her sharp cheekbone and narrow jawline.

She smiled at me.

I smiled back. "How you doin'?" I asked.

Her eyes widened, and her smile grew. She threw a hand over her mouth as she laughed. A soft, enchanting giggle.

I continued smiling. "Happy my question makes you smile and laugh," I said.

She raised her palm and patted the air between us while continuing to laugh. "No, no, no," she struggled to say. "It's just—you have a unique, deep voice. Has anyone ever told you that you sound like Barry White?"

"I may have heard it a few times," I said.

Robby settled a napkin and a dew-dripping glass of Coke in front of her. "Sounds like Barry White and would look like him if he wasn't bald and had more weight on him."

I pointed my thumb at Robby. "See this?" I said. "I've been dealing with it since grade school."

"So, you two went to school together?" she asked.

"Yep. Right here in Tampa," Robby answered.

"Oh, okay."

"My name's Robby, by the way. Let me know if you need anything else," Robby said before looking at me. "Your food will be out shortly, Mr. Barry White. The taller, leaner, bald version."

She giggled. "You have the voice; you have the full beard. If you had more weight, some hair, and was a little shorter, you could go for Barry White's son."

I chuckled, then smiled.

"But," she continued while fixing on my face, "a bald man with a deep voice is a weakness of mine."

"You don't say," I said, leaning toward her. "Because a mocha woman with natural hair and full lips, filling a dress like the one you're wearing, is a weakness of mine."

She glanced away and gently traced her hand down the side of her neck. "You use that line before?" she asked.

"I was just gonna ask you the same thing."

We laughed. I was just about to hit her with one of my best lines, but my phone rang.

"One sec," I told her before removing my phone.

The screen showed a missed call from Keith, my cousin. Not a very close cousin, but close enough to where he felt comfortable calling me when he needed something. Yeah, I was sure he needed something and it could wait, so I figured I'd just call him back later.

"Sorry about that," I said to the woman, placing the phone back inside my pocket. "Now, where were we?"

"You were telling me how you used that same full lips, filling a dress line on other women."

My eyebrows furrowed. "I think we moved past that," I said, half-smiling.

She cocked her head to the side playfully. "Did we?" she asked.

My phone rang again, Keith's number on the screen.

I sighed. "I'm gonna take this," I said before slowly looking her up and down. "Don't wanna but have to."

"Okay."

She smiled and kept her eyes on me as I stood and made my way toward the same door she used to enter. I stepped outside onto the sidewalk and under the cloud-blotted night sky. Pedestrians hoofed the sidewalk and cars whizzed past on the street. I found a spot near the jazz club's entrance and leaned against the wall.

"Yeah, Keith?" I said with the phone to my ear.

"Hi, cuz, I need a favor."

I rolled my eyes. "Naw, really? Here I am thinking you were just calling to check on me."

"You got jokes, but I'm serious, man."

"I was in the middle of sumpin'."

"Look, it's a job."

"You know I don't like doing jobs for family."

"Yeah, yeah, I know. But you're the best at what you do, and this one could be a nice payday."

I sighed but said nothing.

"You'ca put it toward that downtown condo you been saving for."

I inhaled, then slowly exhaled, hoping I wouldn't regret what I was about to do. "What is it? And it betta not be nothing shady," I said.

"No—well, it's a watch."

"A wristwatch?"

"A Rolex. Uncle Eugene gave it to me."

I felt my eyebrows furrow. "Rich Uncle Eugene? I haven't seen him in years. Not since he left Florida. Why would he give you that?"

"He gave it to me when I went to visit him a little while back."

"You hustled it from him?"

"No, no, promise. He told me I can have it and sell it, or do whatever I wanted with it, I promise."

"Uh-huh. How much is the watch worth?" I asked.

"Well, you know it kinda fluctuates depending—"

"Keith, how much?"

"Ahh. Probably forty stacks."

"Whoa! And you lost it?"

"More like someone took it."

I chuckled. "I don't know what Uncle Eugene was thinking, giving you sumpin' like that."

"He didn't care. He has way more where that came from."

"Where's the watch, Keith?"

Keith sighed. "Terrell has it," he answered.

"Wait. The only Terrell I know is the one who wanna be a thug."

I heard Keith shrug through the phone. "Him and a couple of his boys jacked me."

I laughed. I remembered when Terrell was a little snotty nose punk who wanted to be like me. Not exactly sure why he fell off and became a menace to society.

"Yo, not funny," Keith continued.

"Who could've imagined?" I said, tempering myself. "Little Terrell robbing you. You know where he stay?"

"He bounces around, but I know where he's at now."

"Where?"

"Bernini's Pizza."

"Here in Ybor City?"

"Yep."

"Man, that's just up the street from where—wait a minute—you knew I was at my spot."

"I mean, you go there a lot."

I scoffed. "You a trip," I said, shaking my head.

"Will you go get it? I know a man in Sarasota who wanna buy it."

"I got you, but I want half."

"Half?"

"Did I stutter? If you're my client, you're paying like one."

"Whateva, man. I just want it back."

"Guns?" I asked.

"What?"

"Did they have any guns?"

"Yeah, Terrell's boy had one. A skinny guy with a nappy fro and a nappy goatee. He needs to comb that mess."

"But yet they got your watch," I said. "I'm heading there now, half."

I ended the call, then walked back inside.

Robby had his elbows on the bar top, leaning toward the woman, talking.

"So, he came back home after that," is all I heard him say as I approached and took my seat.

"That was quick," Robby said.

"Apparently not quick enough," I said.

"What's that supposed to mean?"

"I didn't know you were a detective in Los Angeles," the woman said.

"That's what I mean," I told Robby.

Robby threw me a dismissal wave. "Your food's about ready," he said before walking toward the kitchen door.

"Hey, just keep it warm for me."

"Alright," Robby said with a shrug.

"I wasn't a detective," I informed the woman.

She winced.

"I passed the detective's exam, but never worked as a detective. Was on LAPD SWAT though."

"Well, aren't you just full of surprises, Mr. Chance Freeman?"

"Oh, he told you my name, too."

She nodded. "Um-hum."

"How long are you going to be here?"

She bit her lower lip and hunched her shoulders. "Not sure."

"Look, I hafta make a quick run, but I'll be back soon, Ms?"

"My name," she said playfully. "I guess you'll find that out when you get back."

"You think that's fair? You knowing my name and me not knowing yours."

She sucked in her lips and shrugged.

"I'll be back soon," I said standing and adjusting my jacket. "And don't believe everything Robby tells you while I'm gone," I continued as I made my way toward the door.

2

My mind was on the mystery woman the entire seven-minute hike to Bernini's Pizza. I stood outside the sparsely crowded hole in the wall, wondering what stories Robby was telling her. Thinking about her plump lips and... I jolted my head. Had to get focused, being I was on a job. A simple job, more like a favor for a family member, but a job nonetheless.

As I entered the restaurant, the aroma from buttery bread and sweet tomato sauce struck my nose. Booths lined the walls and square tables filled the checker-tiled floor.

"How many, sir?" a petite, blonde waitress asked as I scanned the restaurant.

I saw Terrell sitting in a booth near the back wall. He had his hair cut in a low box fade. A small scar underlined the right eye of his scowling face. Next to him sat a skinny man whose reputation did truly proceeded him.

"Yeah, he needs to comb his nappy head and face," I said to myself.

"What was that, sir?" the waitress asked.

"I'm here with my friends," I said, pointing and walking in Terrell's direction.

I caught pieces of conversation and chitchat from patrons as I threaded through tables and approached Terrell's booth. A bald man sat across from Terrell and the guy with the nappy hair.

"Terrell, what's up?" I said.

He winced, then squinted as he fixed on my face. "Chance?" he said, a slight chuckle in his voice.

I shrugged. "Yep. It's me."

Terrell leaned back in his seat. "Haven't seen you in a minute," he said.

I snatched a chair from a nearby table and slid it to the booth. "Saw you sitting and thought we should catch up," I said as I sat in the chair.

On the table sat a basket of garlic knots. I grabbed one and threw it in my mouth.

"Mmmmm."

The nappy-haired man looked me up and down. "Yo, who's this, T?" he asked.

"I grew up with him," Terrell said. "He wrestled in school. People liked him. I even looked up to him back in the day."

"This guy?" the bald man said.

"Yeah. Believe it or not, he was the man."

I nodded, swallowing a morsel of toasty, buttery goodness.

"That's until he became a cop," Terrell continued.

I looked at him.

"Dude's a cop?" Nappy said.

"Used to be," I corrected.

Terrell leaned toward me. "Now he's a lowly private eye."

I ran my tongue across my gums to remove any

remaining debris from the garlic knots, kissing my teeth as I did. "I have my PI license, but I'm not a private investigator."

"Then what are you?" the bald man asked.

"I'm what you'd call a... retrieval consultant."

"Retrieval what?" Nappy said. "That sounds made up."

I noticed the Rolex on Terrell's wrist. "That's a nice watch," I said. "Reminds me of a family heirloom."

Terrell winced. "What?"

"Oh, I forgot. You dropped outta high school and started selling drugs, so you probably don't know what heirloom means." I shared my gaze between Nappy and the bald guy. "And that was way before I became a cop, you know, a bad role model," I said, making air quotes with the last sentence.

Terrell glared at me with bulging eyes and tense jaws. I looked at him with a nonchalant gaze, then kissed my teeth again.

"What you wanna do, Terrell?" Nappy asked.

I eyed him.

"Do you know who you talking to?" Terrell asked me.

I sighed. "Look, I don't have all night," I said, shaking my head. "I know you took that watch from my cousin, so give it to me and we can all go about the rest of our nights."

"Your cousin talks too much, so now it's my watch."

Terrell nodded at Nappy. The skinny man glowered at me, then reached toward his waist and went to stand. Before his butt could leave the seat, I shoved the table into his stomach, then jabbed him in the nose. The bald guy rose from his seat. I rammed the table into his lower abdomen. He arched toward the table as I delivered a devastating right cross to his jaw. The bald man toppled to his side before falling to the floor. Nappy held his nose with his head bowed toward the table. I removed the gun from his hip and yanked him from the booth. As he squirmed on the floor, clenching his bloody nose, I stepped over him and took his seat in the booth right next to Terrell. He stared at me, mouth and eyes wide open.

"The watch," I said with the gun aimed at him under the table.

Terrell removed the watch and handed it to me. I inspected it before placing it into my pocket.

Terrell shrugged. "Now what?"

"Stay away from me, my family, or anyone close to us," I said. "Or it won't end well for you."

Terrell poked his lips and stared at me. I pushed the gun into his side. He grunted.

"Got it?" I said.

"Yeah, yeah I got it."

I ejected the magazine, then pulled the slide, allowing the bullet in the chamber to clink to the floor. Giving Terrell the magazine, I slid from the booth and stepped around his boys on the floor. Terrell told them about my wrestling days but failed to mention I was a golden glove champ back in the day.

"I'll hold on to the gun," I told him.

As I walked to the front of the restaurant, I noticed eyes on me.

I stopped. "Imma cop," I informed everyone before leaving. Which wasn't a hundred percent true, but it wasn't a hundred percent false either.

Once outside, I tossed the gun into a garbage bin and removed my phone. *Got it*, I texted Keith.

The phone rang with a number I didn't recognize.

"Freeman," I answered.

"Ah, Mr. Freeman," a man's voice came through. "I hope it's not too late."

"Who's this?"

"A... a prospect."

"Well, office hours are closed."

The man chuckled. "I understand, but I'll make it worth your while."

"I tell you what, call tomorrow during business hours and we'll talk."

"I'll do that, Mr. Freeman. Talk with you tomorrow."

"Didn't catch your name."

"We'll talk tomorrow."

The call ended. I didn't care for after-hour calls from people I'd never met. Gotta get Darla to have the calls forwarded directly to voicemail, I thought on my way back to the jazz club.

3

I made it back just in time to catch the woman standing from the bar.

"Leaving already?" I asked as I approached.

She winced as if my presence surprised her. "Oh, you," she said, adjusting her dress. "Yeah, I have to go."

I shrugged. "Okay. Let me walk you out."

She looked at me, at the door, then at me again. "Ahh —sure..."

Robby placed a steaming plastic bag on the bar top. "Here's your food," he said to me. "Figured you'd want it to go."

I grabbed the bag. "Thanks, Robby," I said, guiding the woman toward the door.

"Nice to meet you, ma'am," Robby said.

She responded with a quick wave. "Same here."

When we stepped outside, her head was on a swivel.

"You alright?" I asked.

She smiled. "Yeah. Just keeping an eye out for my Uber," she said before looking at her phone. "Should be here any minute now."

"Perfect," I said, extending my hand to her. "Let me hold your phone."

"Why?"

"Trust me."

"That deep voice."

She handed me her phone. I dialed my number and hung up when I felt my phone vibrate inside my pocket.

"Now you have my number," I said, giving her back the phone. "And since you know my name, you can add me to your contacts."

"I'll be sure to do that."

"Speaking of names, you never gave me yours."

She stared at me with a half smile. "Eve," she said. "Eve St—Price, Eve Price."

"Well, nice to meet you, Eve Price," I said while extending my hand.

Her hand seemed to disappear in the expanse of mine as we shook. It was soft and smooth.

"Same here, Chance Freeman."

The heart-shaped diamonds in her bracelet discharged a glint as we released each other's hand. A car pulled to the curb. Eve glanced at the vehicle, then her phone. "Well, that's my ride."

I brushed past her and opened the car's back door.

"Such a gentleman," she said as she slid into the back seat. "Thank you."

"Anytime, babe."

We exchanged smiles. I shut the door, then watched as the car veered into traffic. The glowing taillights shrunk with each passing moment.

Now that's a woman, I thought before walking to my black Cadillac XTS and driving home.

Home was an Aquanaut Drifter 1250 docked at a marina

on Harbour Island. Older model boat, but she held her luxurious appeal. Got it from a rich client at a steal. Equipped with a small kitchen, bathroom, and bedroom, it was all I required for a short-term living arrangement. A specific condo downtown had my name on it, that is, once I saved enough to pay cash for it.

Inside the boat, I placed my bag of food on the counter near the kitchen area. Removing the Rolex from my pocket, I sat on my bed and studied the expensive piece of jewelry.

I felt a grin cross my face. "One step closer to the condo," I uttered to myself.

The next morning, I woke to the sun warming my face. Yawning, I leaned forward and rubbed my eyes. I went to the bathroom, relieved myself, washed up, then lotioned up before heading back into the living area and shrugging into some fresh threads: a khaki button up, short sleeve lapel shirt with navy slacks. While tossing the debris from my dinner into the trash, I grabbed my phone. Two missed messages waited for me on the screen.

Good looking out.

Let's meet up.

Both from Keith. *At one, the park by the aquarium*, I replied.

I slid the Rolex into my pocket and gave my living quarters one last glance before climbing from the boat and clunking across the dock toward my car as the sounds from spilling waves and squawking birds accompanied me.

My first stop was at a drive-through window where I ordered two sausage egg biscuits with hash browns and two coffees. Both with sugar and creamer. The next stop brought me to a small business plaza in Brandon. I parked and exited the car with food and cup carrier in hand. Nestled between a flower shop and a travel agency was my unit. There was no business name on the unit. And that was on purpose. Ninety-five percent of my clients came by referral, and I liked to stay as anonymous as possible. The office space serves as a place to handle back-office stuff and occasionally meet clients. Balancing the food and cup carrier in one hand, I removed my key and unlocked the door.

"You're late," a firm female voice said as I entered.

A small woman with glasses sat at a desk, behind a computer screen, typing.

"Good morning, Darla," I said, shutting and locking the door behind me.

I walked to her desk and placed the food and coffee on top.

"Careful. I'm trying to work here," she said before reaching for the bag. "What'd you get me?"

"A sausage egg biscuit."

She looked at me with her lips poked. "I told you I'm cutting back on that stuff."

"What was I supposed to get you, avocado toast?"

"Yeah," she said, rolling her eyes.

I hired Darla a couple of years back to help with things around the office. And she was very good at it. She had worked as an executive assistant for a big-time law firm downtown but didn't like how the men treated the women. She was efficient, smart, and easy on the eyes. I was lucky to have her. But I never allowed her name, glasses, pretty face, shoulder-length hair, or the way she spoke to fool me. Darla was from around the way, and I knew she was packing.

My phone buzzed. Keith liked the text I sent him earlier.

"Who's that?" Darla asked. "One of your floozies?"

"Keith. Floozies? Somebody's jealous."

Darla scoffed. "Yeah, right."

I grabbed my coffee and biscuit sandwich. "I'll be in my office," I said.

"Oh—someone's here for you."

"Where? In my office?"

"Yeah."

I contorted my lips and cocked my head to the side. "And you just now telling me?"

"He just got here a few minutes before you."

"Well, who is—you know what—I'll find out myself. Oh, can you forward the after-hour calls to voicemail?" I said on the way to my office.

The door was already open. Inside, a fit man wearing a dark gray suit sat in a chair opposite my desk with his legs crossed and his hands clenched in his lap. The man stood as I placed my coffee and sandwich on my desk. His height put him eye level with my shoulders, so I could see the top of his head, which was filled with short, curly hair. Above his lips and around his chin, tiny hairs protruded from his light-brown skin.

"Mr. Freeman," he said, extending his hand while smiling with some of the straightest pearly whites I'd ever seen.

"Yes, and you are?" I asked as we shook hands.

"Patrick Stevenson. I called you last night."

"Right," I said, circling behind my desk. "Sorry if I was abrupt, but it was after hours, and I was working a case."

Stevenson shrugged. "If you're as good as I hear, then I guess you can afford to be abrupt."

"So, who referred me?"

"Charles West."

"Chuck? Really?"

Stevenson nodded.

Charles West was the rich client in Miami who sold me my houseboat. Nice man. He and I were on good terms.

I gestured for Stevenson to sit as I did the same. I placed my elbows on the desk and clenched my hands together. "So how do you know Chuck?" I asked.

"Years ago, we worked a deal together."

I nodded.

Stevenson adjusted in his chair and leaned forward while tugging his blazer's lapels. "Look, Mr. Freeman," he said, "time is of the essence. I have a job for you and I'm willing to pay a lot for its completion."

"Okay," I said, reclining in my chair. "What do you need me to retrieve?"

"A person."

I chuckled. "Mr. Stevenson, I'm in the business of collecting things, not people. I'm sure Chuck mentioned that."

"Yes, he made it clear you specialize in the procurement of personal articles, but I don't want you to collect the individual. Just locate them."

"Why me? Sounds like a missing person's case." I hunched my shoulders. "Why not just go to the police?"

"The situation is... well, the situation is delicate."

I scoffed and shook my head. "Delicate?"

"I'll pay fifty thousand up front and another fifty once the job is complete."

I leaned forward. Now he really had my attention.

"One hundred thousand?" I asked to confirm.

Stevenson nodded. "I'll even throw in an extra ten percent for any supplies you may need."

I drummed my fingers on the desk and felt my eyes squint. My experience taught me when something sounded too good to be true, it probably was. But then I felt a nudge from the condo owner inside of me, urging me to take a chance. You only live once. Plus, I'd seen rich people spend a lot more money on things less suspicious.

"When was the last time you saw this person?" I asked.

"Does that mean you're taken the job?" Stevenson asked.

"Probably."

"Well, then, three weeks ago. New York."

"You live in New York?"

"I do a lot of business in New York, so I have a home there, yes."

"New York? What makes you think this person is in Tampa?"

"The previous contractor I hired tracked them here."

"So, you already hired someone?"

Stevenson shook his head. "They're no longer working for me. We had a disagreement."

I stared at him in a moment of awkward silence. "Your case seems complicated, Mr. Stevenson," I said.

"I guess you can say that."

Looking at him, I reclined in my chair and rubbed my chin. I wanted to give the impression that I was possibly considering passing on the job.

"One hundred thousand," I said. "Just to locate this person?"

Stevenson nodded. "That's it," he said, a slight chuckle in his voice.

"Alright. Half up front, and I'm going to need details about this missing individual," I said while reaching for a pen and pad on my desk.

"Certainly," Stevenson said, as he reached into his blazer's inside pocket and removed a check. He slid it across the desk. "That's half," he continued before reaching into his opposite pocket and producing a photo. "And this is her," he said, sliding it toward me.

The picture was upside down. As I grabbed the photo, I spun it right side up, and my eyes widened when I recognized the person in the picture.

"That's my wife," Stevenson said. "Eve."

4

Eve looked the same in the photo as she did the night before at the jazz club. Except in the picture, she was wearing what appeared to be a white wedding dress.

"Your wife?" I asked, wanting to make sure I heard him correctly.

"Yes," Stevenson said. "That picture was taken at our wedding two years ago."

"Eve? Eve Stevenson?"

Stevenson chuckled. "Yes. And I would like you to find her."

"I don't get it. You know she's here in Tampa. Why not just call her? She is your wife."

"It's not that easy. She's already changed her number twice."

I shook my head. "Don't know, Mr. Stevenson. Sounds like she doesn't want to be found."

"You work for her or me?"

"Neither at this point. Not until I have more details at least," I said while sliding the check back toward Stevenson.

He sighed. "What else do you need to know?"

"Any idea why she would come to Tampa?"

Stevenson hunched his shoulder. "My only guess is she's familiar with the area. Her family used to vacation here a lot when she was younger."

"Speaking of family, does she have any here?"

"Not that I know of," Stevenson said while folding his arms. "Which is why I'm hiring you. To figure all this out."

"What happened in New York three weeks ago?"

"What do you mean?"

"You said the last time you saw your wife was in New York three weeks ago. What happened before she headed south?"

"That's personal. Suffice it to say, we had a minor disagreement."

"You certainly have a lot of disagreements, Mr. Stevenson."

"Do you want the job or not?"

Part of me wanted to say no. This whole situation stunk of complications. Not to mention it bordered on a conflict of interest, considering I had already met Eve and all. But the condo owner inside of me didn't want to pass on the chance to make a hundred grand.

I nodded. "I'll take the job," I said.

"Great," Stevenson said, clapping his palms together, then sliding the check back toward me.

"Is there anything else I should know, Mr. Stevenson?"

Stevenson shrugged his lips and stood. "Nope," he said, adjusting his blazer. "You have my number, so let me know as soon as you find anything."

"Of course," I said while standing.

As I circled around my desk, Stevenson exited my office. I stood just outside the office door and watched as he exited the unit. When the door shut behind him, Darla stared at me. She adjusted her glasses as if she was expecting an explanation. I shrugged, then returned to my desk. I usually told Darla everything, and this situation would be no different. Just wasn't ready to tell her right then.

I ate my sandwich and finished half of my coffee while considering how to approach the case. Giving Mrs. Eve Price, or rather Eve Stevenson, a call would probably be a good place to start. It could be a breach of her trust, though. Not to mention a breach of my client Mr. Stevenson's trust. I thought maybe I'd just have a conversation with her and see what's going on. If the water was too murky, I'd back out of the job without receiving the final payment. I felt good about that plan.

"Darla," I called as I exited my office.

She looked at me.

"I'm stepping out. Can you do me a favor, sweetheart?"

She cocked her head to the side and poked her lips. "What is it, Chance?"

"Can you find out as much as you can about Patrick Stevenson? And his wife, Eve Stevenson. Try Eve Price, too. I believe that's her maiden name."

"Where're you goin'?" Darla asked.

"The bank. Call me when you have something," I said before locking and shutting the door on my way out.

I eased behind the wheel of my Caddy, then pushed the ignition button, and she purred to life. The drive to the bank took less than ten minutes, and it took about the same to get inside and deposit the check. A smile arched on my face when I looked at the deposit receipt and saw my account fifty thousand dollars fatter. Once back inside my car, I figured it was time to start the job, so I removed my phone and dialed Eve's number.

"Hello," a male's voice answered.

"Sorry," I said. "Think I dialed the wrong number."

"Are you looking for Eve Stevenson?"

"Maybe. Why you ask?"

"Who are you?"

"Just some good-looking guy she picked up last night. Who are you? Where's Eve?"

"Detective Greg Hiller with the Tampa PD."

I winced at the phone. Many questions flooded my mind, but I kept cool and listened.

"Not sure where Eve is," Hiller continued. "But since you're one of our only leads, maybe you can answer some questions for us."

"I'll think about it," I said before ending the call. My eyebrows furrowed as I held and stared at the phone. "What's goin' on?" I said aloud.

5

Greg Hiller. I worked with the Tampa PD almost every day and the name didn't ring a bell. So, I figured I'd pay a cop buddy of mine a visit down at the station. When I arrived at the station, the officer at the front desk immediately greeted me.

"What's goin' on, Chance?" he said as he buzzed me in.

"What's up, Jeff?" I said, opening the door. "Just another day in paradise for me. How's the wife and boys?"

"Good, man. Everybody's good."

I nodded. "Good. Hey, is Ed around?"

"Yeah, I think I saw him earlier."

"Thanks," I said before passing through the door.

I entered a large room filled with desks, many occupied by officers typing away at their computers. A few of the officers engaged in conversations with civilians sitting opposite their desks. On my way to a glass-walled office near the back, I passed some desks and dodged a handcuffed man arguing with his police escort. The office blinds were closed, so I knocked on the door with the plaque, *Sgt. Edward*

McCoach. After five knocks and no response, I opened the door and peeked inside to find the office empty.

"Hi, Chance," a soft voice said to my back.

I turned and behind me stood a tall, slender woman in a police uniform. No name tag. She wore her hair pixied with curls, and her dimples cut into her almond-toned cheeks as she smiled at me.

"Hi," I said, trying to remember her name and confused at how I could forget such a woman's name.

"Looking for Sergeant McCoach?" she asked.

"Yes, I am, pretty thang."

She giggled. "Pretty thang. I have a name, you know."

"Of course you do."

"What is it?"

I chuckled. "C'mon now."

"You don't remember. You're something else, Chance Freeman."

"Remind me."

She winced at my request. "It won't be that easy," she said. "Follow me."

We threaded across the floor and into a hallway. In a huddle room at the end of the hall, we found McCoach, in uniform, alone. His buzzed-cut head bobbed as he wrote on a whiteboard.

"Sergeant McCoach," the female officer said.

McCoach turned to us. His bushy eyebrows furrowed, and his thick mustache arched above his pouty lips. As long as I'd known him, he'd always had a gruff demeanor but was a good cop and friend.

"Chance is here to see you," the lady officer continued.

"Thanks," McCoach said in his husky voice.

She smiled at me. "And don't tell him my name," she said before leaving the room.

"That lady's something else," I said, walking between a line of chairs on my way to McCoach. "Don't know why a woman like that would want to hang around a police station with a bunch of middle-aged white men like yourself."

McCoach shook his head and chuckled. "You said that the last two times you saw her," he said before turning back to the whiteboard. "What's going on, Freeman? I have a briefing to prepare for."

"Was wondering if you could help me sort out some details on my case."

"What case?"

"I'm looking for someone."

"You find things, not people," McCoach said as he wrote on the board.

"This case is a little different."

McCoach faced me. "Different how?"

"Well... It's..."

As I struggled to explain myself, the door opened, and a group of officers entered the room.

"Let's talk later," McCoach said.

"Morning, Detective Sergeant," one officer said as he sat in a chair upfront.

McCoach nodded.

I found a chair near the back of the room as more people entered. McCoach went through roll call. There were only about nine officers in the room, so it wasn't long before he called, "Detective Hiller."

"Present," an athletically built man said.

Unlike most of the other officers in the room, I'd never seen him before. He had tanned skin and slicked-back, dirty-blond hair. Looked like he spent more time on the beach than in the police station.

After roll call, McCoach had every officer give an update

on their case. I leaned back in my chair and paid little attention until he called on Hiller.

"Sir," Hiller said to McCoach. "I've closed the Langford case. Turns out their missing daughter was just a rebellious runaway. She returned home when she ran short on cash. The Dunn case appears to be a situation where the husband doesn't want to be found. Think we have the identity and location of his mistress. I imagine we'll have that one wrapped up by the end of the week."

"Hey, new guy," a woman officer said to Hiller. "What about the case that came in a few days ago?"

"Yeah, I was getting to that one. Looks like a case of the wife just not wanting to be found but may be more complicated," Hiller said.

McCoach's forehead wrinkled. "What makes you so sure?" he asked.

Hiller hunched his shoulders. "Well, according to the private investigator," he said, looking at the ceiling, then tapping his index finger against his chin. "What's his name? Ahh, Jacob Finley. When he filed the missing person's report, he stated the husband was looking for her, but she didn't act like she wanted to be found—by her husband, at least."

"Wow. No one wants to be married these days," the female officer said.

"Don't worry, someone will marry you," one male officer told her.

"Just like I'm sure there's some woman desperate enough to marry you."

The group laughed.

"Okay, everyone, calm down," McCoach said. "What makes you say there're more complications?" he asked, directing his question at Hiller.

"Not entirely sure, just seems—strange," Hiller said. "We knew the motel where she was staying, thanks to Finley. So, we thought it would be a good idea to check on her ourselves to confirm if a crime was actually committed. But when we arrived there this morning, we found her door open and the room disheveled, like she left in a hurry."

I sat up in my chair.

"She left behind some clothes and a few personal items, including her phone," Hiller continued. "The motel clerk said she never checked out."

McCoach cuffed his chin. "Interesting. Any more leads?"

Hiller shrugged. "I've reached out to Finley but haven't been able to get him," he said before sighing. "I was planning on running by his office today." Hiller wagged his index finger in the air. "There is another possible lead. As we were storing her phone into evidence, it rang. I answered the call and a man with a deep voice said he was looking for Eve."

"Eve's the missing person?" the female officer asked.

"Yeah. Eve Stevenson. But anyway, I guess the man met her the night before."

"A booty call!" one officer blurted. "You answered her booty call."

The group laughed, and I took it as my cue to leave, so I stood from my chair and headed for the door.

"Everybody, quiet," McCoach said. "Have we identified this man?"

"Not yet," Hiller said. "But I have the guys looking into the number."

When I made it to the door, McCoach noticed. I gave him a hand gesture that suggested I'd talk with him later, then exited the room.

6

While sitting at a red light, I removed my phone and called Darla.

"Don't have any information on the Stevensons yet," she answered. "Was just about to look into it."

"Before you do that, I have a different person," I said.

"Okay. Who?"

"See if you can find a phone number and address for Jacob Finley."

"Finley?"

"Yeah. He's a PI."

"Alright. I'll see what I can find."

"Thanks, baby doll."

"Chance, we've had this talk already. Darla is my name."

"Fine. Thanks, Darla."

"Much better. I'll let you know what I find."

The call ended, and I continued my drive to the jazz club. When I arrived, a few cars pulled in around the back of the building. I parked the Caddy at the curb, then walked along the building's side. Cigarette smoke struck my nose when I made it halfway to the back. A group of men hummed while unloading footlockers from a van and carrying them into the building's back doors.

"You're a little early, aren't you, Chance?" one of them said.

"What, no shows before lunchtime?" I asked.

The man chuckled. "Naw, man, I'm afraid not," he said between cigarette puffs.

"Is Robby in yet?"

"Yeah, he's in the kitchen."

"I thought you were quitting," I said, pointing at the cigarette in his hand.

He shrugged. "I did—but you know—old habits. Like you and women."

I shook my head. "Watch it now," I said on my way through the back doors.

A dark hallway welcomed me. At the end of the hall, there was a stage and a dance floor. I continued across the dark, quiet space to the bar top. Clanking and ruffling flowed from the kitchen. I knocked on the bar top.

"Robby!"

The noise stopped. Seconds later, the kitchen door swung open, and Robby walked through.

"Chance. What're you doing here?" he said.

"Need to ask you something."

"Okay, go ahead."

"You remember that woman last night?"

Robby smiled. "Oh, yeah. How'd things go with you two?" he asked.

"Nothing went with us. We exchanged numbers. She got in her ride, then we went our separate ways."

Robby kissed his teeth. "Really?"

"Yep. Really."

"Imma check the front camera's video to make sure," Robby joked.

I pointed at him. "Do that. And send a copy to me."

Robby paused and stared at me. "You're serious. What's going on?"

I glanced around the jazz club, then waved Robby toward the kitchen door. "C'mon, let's go to the back and talk," I said, circling the bar top.

I spent five minutes catching Robby up with the situation.

"Boy, you sure know how to pick em," he said.

"Don't start," I told him. "I didn't pick her; she just happened to be here the same time as me."

"Why didn't you tell McCoach about her? He'll have your back."

"I'll let him know. Didn't want to complicate the situation."

"How complicated you think it's gonna be when he finds out on his own? They already have your phone number."

"It's a burner number."

"Either way, just a matter of time before he finds out. Might as well be from you."

I nodded. "I know. Hey, did she mention anything to you when I stepped away?"

Robby shrugged his lips. "No," he said, shaking his head. "I did most of the talking."

My phone vibrated. I removed it and saw a missed call from Darla.

"I hafta get outta here," I said on my way to the kitchen's door. "Don't forget to send me that video footage."

"I gotcha," Robby said as I exited the kitchen.

On the way to my car, I returned Darla's call. She gave me the address to Jacob Finley's private investigation practice in St. Petersburg, even texted me a picture of him. I drove on I-275 for twenty-seven minutes, then on I-175 for an additional two minutes before arriving in downtown St. Petersburg. Traffic was smooth, with only a few vehicles on the road. As I cruised along 4th Street, palm trees, shopping and restaurant outlets, and the occasional ten to twenty-story building surrounded me on either side. I parked at the curb across the street from Finley's office. It was a small, one-story industrial building sitting somewhat off to itself.

I made my way across the street, and as I approached the front door, I noticed it was ajar.

I knocked on the door. "Finley, Jacob Finley."

A loud thump followed by footsteps shuffling wafted to the door. I peeked through the opening and a rotten odor swept across my face. I knew the smell. It was the scent of death. I quickly entered a small receptionist foyer, where a desk greeted me. Behind the desk, a contemporary sitting area sat surrounded by offices and a conference room. A man lay on the floor near the sitting area. I raced to him and quickly recognized Jacob Finley.

"Finley," I said, but he didn't answer.

I'd seen many dead bodies and was positive I was looking at one. He had two bullet holes in his chest and one in his head. The blood had dried to his skin. As I kneeled to further inspect the body, a figure zipped from an office and down a hall near the back of the building.

"Hey!" I shouted as I gave chase.

Dashing into the hall, the figure shoved open the door at the opposite end. I increased my pace and shouldered through the door before it closed. Stumbling into an alley, I looked up as a garbage bin eclipsed the sun and descended toward me. The trash container struck my side and knocked me off balance. I smacked into a wall and trash from the bin littered the alley. As I pushed from the wall, I got a good look at the figure.

A man in a hoodie with a face band covering his mouth and nose stood in front of me, four inches shorter than my height. He flicked open a knife and rushed me. I raised my fist and my survival and boxing instincts kicked in. As the man thrust the blade at my chest, I parried his hand before throwing two jabs in quick succession. Both attacks struck his jaw, then out of pure muscle memory, I threw a left cross and connected with his right eye. My attacker stumbled backward, and his back slapped into a wall. With my fist raised, I shuffled toward him. He feinted a knife jab. I flinched, briefly leaving my left side open. The man slashed the blade and grazed my left shoulder. I hit him with another cross, then shoved him. My opponent raced through the alley with me behind him. As we approached the main road, the man knocked over a garbage bin. I dodged it but slipped and fell to one knee. In the couple of seconds it took me to recover, the man turned a corner at the intersecting street.

When I exited the alley, he was nowhere to be found.

"Great!" I grumbled, grabbing my left shoulder and inspecting it. My fingers brushed over a minor cut with a thin coat of blood. "That punk cut my shirt. What's goin' on here?"

I pondered the question during my short walk back to the car. Once inside, I immediately removed my phone and dialed.

"We need to talk!" I said before the person could greet me.

7

"What is it? You have something for me?" Stevenson asked.

"Yeah, I have something," I said. "Questions."

Stevenson released a nervous chuckle through the phone. "I've told you everything you need—"

"No, you didn't. Was Jacob Finley the PI you hired?"

"Well, Chance, I don't believe—"

"Stop playing with me, Stevenson. Yes or no."

"Yes, but I've already told you I hired someone."

"Finley was based in Florida. That means you already knew Eve was in Florida when you hired him."

"Was?"

"Yeah, was. Finley's dead."

Stevenson gasped. "What? Oh, my. How?"

"Looked like a professional hit."

Stevenson said nothing.

"You knew Eve was in Florida before hiring Finley? How?" I asked.

Stevenson sighed. "I had someone following her in New York. That investigator learned she was seeing a guy in Tampa."

"Wow."

"I know. Can you believe her?"

"Her? What about you? If you put as much time, money, and energy into understanding your wife as you do spying on her, you wouldn't have this problem."

Stevenson chuckled. "If you say so," he said. "Anyhow, the man she cheated with would come to New York and visit her a couple of times a month. I wanted to know more about the guy, but the investigator I hired in New York didn't work out of state. That's when I employed Finley. He dug up some information on the guy and provided surveillance when I needed it. So, when Eve left New York, Finley confirmed she met up with her little boy toy."

"Hmm. What was the disagreement between you and Finley?"

Stevenson drew in a long breath before slowly exhaling. "I may have made an unsavory suggestion, but I didn't mean it."

I shook my head at the phone. "Wishing death on you wife and her lover," I said. "Have to admit, Mr. Stevenson, this isn't looking good for you."

The line fell silent.

"Why did Eve leave New York? What did you two disagree on?" I said, putting specific emphasis on disagree.

"Like I told you before, it's personal."

"This whole situation smells. I'm seriously considering backing out of the job and handing everything over to my cop buddies."

"Wait, look, all I need from you is to locate her and you'll have an additional fifty grand. Plus another ten for any incidentals."

The condo owner inside of me once again reared his acquisitive head.

"I'll find her, but I need to know why she left New York to begin with."

Stevenson sighed into the phone. "All right, I'll tell you," he said. "Just not over the phone. Let's meet somewhere."

"Your day's pretty open?"

"Yeah."

"Okay. I'll call you back a little later with a place."

"Sounds good. Hey, did the cops find Finley's body?"

"They will," I said before ending the call. Figured the less Stevenson knew, the better, since he was my client, and I didn't trust him.

The drive back to Tampa took me a little longer on account of traffic. During the entire ride, I wrestled with the thought of calling McCoach and telling him about Finley's dead body and all the events leading up to it, but ultimately, I decided it wasn't the right time. The situation had gotten messy, and I was slap in the middle of it. I stopped at a popular burger joint's drive thru near downtown and ordered a double cheeseburger and Coke. The food remained untouched until I made it to my destination—a sparsely crowded park just twenty yards from The Florida Aquarium. Finding parking was easy. I grabbed my burger and Coke before exiting the car, then strolled across the parking lot until I passed two immense palm trees and ended up in an open grassy field. I surveyed the area but didn't see Keith. Taking a bite from my burger, I circled a small playground, then found a seat at an empty bench.

Children's laughter mixed with parents' admonishments for safety chattered the air. I finished my burger and made it halfway through my Coke before I saw Keith. He grinned on his way to me. I ejected from the bench as he approached. Keith stood a few inches shorter than me. We had similar body builds and features except he was thinner and sported a faux hawk and fade.

"Hey, what's up, cuz?" he said, smiling.

"Don't what's up cuz me," I said. "You betta had not hustled Uncle Eugene outta his watch."

"I told you I didn't. He gave it to me. You know how rich people can get—sometimes they just give stuff away."

"Uh-huh, I bet," I said, clasping my cousin's hand, then pulling him in for a hug. "Come here, man. Haven't seen you in a while."

"Yeah, it's been a minute," Keith said as we released our embrace. His eyes squinted as he pointed to my left shoulder. "What happened?"

"Nothing, just a scratch," I said.

Keith shrugged.

"So, when do you plan on meeting your buyer?" I asked.

"Today. I can have your cut to you tomorrow."

With my head on a swivel, I reached into my pocket and removed the Rolex. "Half," I said while handing the watch to Keith.

Keith smiled as he placed the watch in his own pocket.

"Half," I repeated.

"Yeah, yeah, I got it," Keith said. "I hafta go if I wanna catch the buyer today. Whatchu doin the rest of the day?"

"My afternoon's full. Gotta client to meet."

We fist bumped.

"I'll let you know when I have it, cuz," Keith said before making his way across the park.

"You betta," I said.

When Keith disappeared from my view, I removed my phone and dialed Stevenson on the way to my car. He answered on the second ring, then I gave him the address to a diner in Valrico and told him to meet me there in an hour.

8

Thirty minutes later, I pulled into the diner's parking lot. Since I didn't trust Stevenson, I wanted to be early to case the place. I removed my Smith & Wesson M&P and its magazine from my glove compartment. After confirming the chamber was clear and inserting the magazine, I emerged from the car and stuffed the handgun in the back of my pants and made sure my shirt hid it. Once inside the diner, I sat at a table near the back. A petite waitress with short, curly hair checked on me periodically. Each time, I told her I didn't want anything and was waiting for a friend. But after twenty-five minutes of us doing that dance, I finally asked her to bring me a Coke. With small sips, I finished the soda twenty minutes later and there was no sign of Stevenson.

The waitress approached my table. "When is your friend coming?" she asked.

I hunched my shoulders. "They were supposed to be here like fifteen minutes ago." I smiled at her. "But I do appreciate you keeping me company, sweetheart."

She smiled. "Want a refill?"

I shook my head. "I'm good."

"Can I get you anything else?"

"Not right now. How much do I owe you?"

She threw me a dismissal wave. "It's on me."

"Why, thank you," I said, standing from the table.

"I hope you find your friend," the waitress said.

I shrugged before stepping to her and leaning toward her ear. "I think I like my new friend better," I whispered.

She giggled. I smiled at her, then eased toward the door. I glanced back and gave her one more smile as I exited the diner. On the way to my car, I dialed Stevenson. The phone rang until I got his voicemail. I ended the call before Stevenson's voice asked me to leave a message. I waited in my car for another ten minutes. Stevenson didn't show, so I left for my office. On the way, I called him a second time and once again got his voicemail.

"I don't know what he's tryna pull," I uttered to myself as I ended the call.

A ginger, garlicky aroma with a hint of soy sauce struck my nose as I entered the office. A steaming container sat on Darla's desk. The bathroom door thumped closed, and she emerged from the hall.

"You're back," she said on the way to her desk. "I was just about to have a late lunch. Would've ordered you something but figured you'd already ate."

"I did," I said with a sigh.

Darla stopped walking and pivoted away from her desk. "Everything alright?" she asked while walking toward me.

I pursed my lips and cocked my head to the side.

"Do you need to tell me something?" she asked.

I shrugged. "You know, baby doll. Just the normal hiccups cases like this bring."

Darla rolled her eyes and sighed before glancing at the floor, then my left shoulder. "Is that what that is?" she asked, pointing at the minor injury. "A hiccup? And no, I don't know. You left without telling me about this case."

"Well, we're about to change that now," I said, placing my hand on her back and guiding her toward her desk.

I spent eleven minutes telling Darla everything while sitting near her desk as she inspected and cleaned my cut.

"Well, you had a busy day," she said before shaking her head. "You and these women."

I said nothing, just flinched as she pressed a bandage on my cut.

"The good thing is," she continued, "you had a big payday today."

I felt a smile arch on my face. "Yeah, it's nice," I said while nodding.

"Good for you," Darla said before slapping my injury.

"Ouch! What was that for?"

"Not telling me sooner. I thought we were a team."

"We are a team, baby doll. I just wasn't sure what was goin' on. Still not. And this is good for us. You know I got you."

"Good," Darla said, standing from her desk with the first aid box in hand. "That means I may not have to work for you much longer." She walked toward the bathroom.

"You don't mean that, baby doll."

"Why do you insist on calling me that?"

I chuckled to myself as Darla disappeared into the bathroom. She came back a minute later, drying her hands with a paper towel as she sat back at her desk.

"Did you find anything on Eve or Stevenson today?" I asked her.

She shook her head while opening her container of food. "Nothing more than you already know, but I'll dig deeper now, obviously."

I nodded. "Also, Imma need you to work from home. Just until we get a handle on this situation."

Darla shrugged. "I get it," she said while sticking a fork into her stir fry chicken. She glanced at me. "You're gonna let McCoach know?" she asked before taking a bite.

"I will."

Darla stared at me.

"I will," I repeated.

"Okay."

"I know I asked to have the after-hour calls forwarded to voicemail—"

"They're still going to you," Darla said between chews.

"Good. And since you'll be keeping a low profile, have all the calls forwarded to me."

"You're sure?"

"Yep."

While Darla ate her late lunch, I went to my office and locked my desk and file cabinet drawers. When she finished, we locked up the rest of the office and I tailed her home. She lived in a luxury apartment building downtown with a concierge, plenty of restaurants and shops nearby, and security.

Parked at the curb across the street, I watched as she entered her parking garage. She called me to confirm she had made it to her unit. After leaving Darla's place, I drove five blocks to my future condo. It was a luxury building much like Darla's, expect it sat near the water. I eased the Caddy next to the curb, then watched the building. It helped me to think. My phone vibrated with a text from Robby.

I only sent the part where you helped her in the car.

I played the video below his text message. It showed me opening the car for Eve, us staring at each other, then me shutting the door and the car pulling off. I dropped my phone in the passenger seat and continued in my thoughts.

After five minutes, I pulled off. On the way home, I stopped for a pizza. I liked pizza because it meant I didn't have to do any dishes.

With the case being so shaky, I decided to drive the boat to another dock I rented about a nautical mile away from my primary marina. It was for emergencies and only a few people knew about it. I arrived there in under twenty minutes and secured my boat for the night.

After finishing my pizza, I called Stevenson, but again only got his voicemail. I tossed the phone on my bed, and everything else, I placed on the stand next to the bed, then went to the bathroom to wash up. When I made it back to the bedroom, my phone vibrated. A text message displayed on the screen.

I got all the cash, Keith's message read. *Same time, same place tomorrow?*

That should work, I replied before connecting the phone to its charger.

I lay on the bed, and three minutes later, my eyelids shut.

9

I woke to my phone ringing, my office forwarding number displayed on the screen.

"Hello," I answered.

"Freeman," McCoach's husky voice came on the line. "You still in bed?"

I groaned as I adjusted my position. "Well, it is just a quarter after eight."

McCoach scoffed. "I keep forgetting you work for yourself," he said. "A guy like me has to be up early, even after a late night."

"Caught another case last night?"

"I'm always catching cases, but yes."

I leaned forward and twisted to where my legs hung over the bedside and my feet rested on the chilled floor. "Oh, really?"

"Yeah. We had a body, but it was out of our jurisdiction, so had to play ping-pong with Saint Pete PD all evening."

I said nothing.

"Then this morning I thought of you."

I stayed quiet

"You came to me for help with your case, but we never talked about it. Figured I'd reach out to you before I got too busy today."

I sighed. "Yeah, we need to talk."

"I bet we do."

"You had breakfast yet?" I asked.

"Not yet."

"Let's meet for breakfast. In an hour."

"Sure. Jay's Cafe?"

"That's our place."

Fifty minutes later, I pulled into Jay's Cafe's parking lot. The cafe was a dark yellow, one-story stucco house converted into a restaurant. I placed my gun in the glove compartment and exited the car. Once inside the cafe, I spotted McCoach sitting in a booth with a steaming cup of coffee to his mouth. I threaded through the sparsely occupied dining room and slid into the booth across from him.

"You ordered yet?" I asked.

McCoach shook his head. "Just the coffee," he said. "Was waiting for you." He pointed at the table. "The waitress left a menu."

"I don't need it," I said. "I'm g'ttin' my usual."

McCoach shrugged. "I told her," he said before chuckling. "But didn't protest when she insisted on leaving it in case you wanted it."

"You always allowed women to push you around."

"And you always allowed women to get you in trouble."

I smirked. "Well, that's not always a bad thing," I said.

We both laughed.

McCoach took another sip of coffee. "So, tell me about this case you're working."

"It's a mess and doesn't look good."

"I bet."

I adjusted in my seat. "Where to start?" I sighed. "Yesterday I took a job from a wealthy, annoying, and kinda shady guy."

"Who?"

"Stevenson. Patrick Stevenson."

McCoach's eyebrows rose. "Have you seen him today?" he asked.

My eyebrows furrowed. "No, but interesting you asked because I was supposed to meet him yesterday and he ghosted me. Why? Do you know him?"

"I don't know him, but I know where he is."

I winced. "What? Where?"

"The hospital."

"The hospital? As in Tampa General Hospital?"

McCoach nodded. "Exactly," he said. "He was involved in a hit-and-run last night. An officer on the scene briefed me. Stevenson's pretty banged up."

My gaze fell to the table before flicking back to McCoach's face. "How did it happen?" I asked.

"A silver SUV ran a red light. Totaled his car. He's lucky to be alive."

"What about the driver in the SUV?"

McCoach shrugged. "Don't know. They fled the scene."

Once again, my gaze fell to the table.

"What's going on, Chance?" McCoach asked.

I looked at him and sighed. "I'll tell you what I know. But like I said, it's a mess, and doesn't look good."

It took me sixteen minutes to tell McCoach what I knew, and to show him the video Robby sent me. It would've taken less if not for the waitress' interruptions, but at that point, I had a cup of coffee in front of me and both McCoach and I had ordered our food.

McCoach placed his cup on the table after taking a sip. "The video shows you weren't the last person with Mrs. Stevenson when she left the jazz club," he said.

I nodded. "That's right."

McCoach cuffed his chin, then patted his cheek with that hand's index finger. "So, when you arrived at Finley's office, he was already dead and someone else was at the scene?"

I glanced around the cafe, then leaned toward McCoach. "Yes," I said, almost in a whisper. "He was dead."

"So, the other person there killed him?"

I shook my head. "I wouldn't say so. Finley was shot—looked like a professional hit. The guy I tussled with had a knife. He had some moves and all, but he didn't strike me as a stone-cold killer. Also, Finley had been dead for a while before I got there."

"What makes you say that?"

"His blood had already dried. Did your guys find any gun shells?"

McCoach shook his head.

"Yeah. I think whoever killed Finley is careful and wouldn't've made the mistake of returning to the scene."

"But we know for sure you and this other guy were there," McCoach said.

"What does that mean?"

"You said it yourself, Freeman. It doesn't look good."

"But you believe me, right?"

"Of course, but—"

The waitress approached and placed our plates on the table. "Anything else I can get for either of you?" she asked.

McCoach shook his head.

"No thanks," I told her.

She walked away, and I turned back to McCoach.

"But what?" I asked.

"There's procedures around these things. You know that," McCoach said.

"I'm gonna figure out what's going on."

McCoach took another sip of coffee. "I hope so. Hiller comes across a bit flaky, but it won't take him long to figure out you're involved. Your number is on both Stevenson's and Eve's phones. How long do you think it'll take him to find out it's your number?"

"Probably a while," I said.

McCoach's eyebrows furrowed.

"It's a burner," I continued.

McCoach sighed. "I didn't hear that," he said. "My point is, it won't take him long to realize Stevenson hired you." He sucked in his lips and looked up as if a thought came to him. "How much is he paying you, anyway?"

I shrugged. "That's client privilege."

McCoach chuckled. "Yeah, I bet it is. Well, I'm the Detective Sergeant on this case. That means you don't have much time to sort this out. I'd say you have twelve hours."

"Starting when?" I asked.

"Twenty minutes ago."

"Well, I guess I better eat fast."

We finished our food and left the cafe. McCoach reiterated he could only keep the heat off me until ten o'clock that night. And since he didn't owe me that, I thanked him and told him I'd be in touch soon.

The first stop I wanted to make was the hospital. I dialed Darla on my way there.

"I was wondering when you were going to call me," she said when she answered the phone.

"Why you wondering about me?" I asked in a teasing manner. "Thought you'd take advantage of this remote work situation—you know, lie around in your pajamas and eat cereal."

"You're half right. I'm in my pajamas, but not doing the cereal thing today."

"Well, I just wanted to call and check on you."

"Ahh, how sweet of you."

"I told McCoach."

"Really? How'd that go?"

"To put it short, I have less than twelve hours to get a grip on this thing."

"Hm. That was very lenient of him."

"Trust me, I'm not complaining," I said.

"Where are you heading now?"

"To the hospital. Stevenson is in the hospital."

Darla scoffed into the phone. "What's going on?"

"He was involved in a hit-and-run."

"It's getting stranger by the minute. But speaking of Stevenson, I did a little more research this morning, and did you know he owns a lot of properties in New York and New Jersey?"

I shrugged at the wheel. "He mentioned he does a lot of business in New York, so?"

"So why does he use various LLCs? I checked out five of his properties and two are in a corporation, two more in another, and the last property is in one by itself."

"A bit strange, but many business owners operate various LLCs."

Darla sighed. "Right, but two properties are literally up

the street from one another and they're under different company names."

"That's a bit more unusual. You thinking shell companies?"

"Probably."

"Well, I'll be sure to ask Stevenson about that."

"Alright. I'll keep poking around," Darla said before ending the call.

After finding a spot in the hospital's parking garage, I took my gun from the glove compartment and stuffed it in the back of my pants as I emerged from the car. With the way the case was going, I wanted to be prepared for anything.

Inside the hospital, a full-figured woman sat behind the front receptionist counter. She smiled as I approached.

"You're here to see someone?" she asked.

"I am. But seeing your pretty face just made my day."

The receptionist's smile grew. "Who are you here to see?" she asked before glancing at the computer screen in front of her.

"Stevenson. Patrick Stevenson."

She stared at the screen while dragging and clicking her computer mouse. After a moment, she looked at me and said, "He's on the fourth floor. Room four twelve."

I smiled. "Thanks, beautiful."

She gave me a visitor's sticker, then I rode the elevator to the fourth floor and strolled the empty hall, following the signs to room four twelve. Stevenson had a room to himself. He lay on the bed with bandages wrapped around his head and bruises on his face. As I walked closer, I noticed his eyes were closed. Thinking he was unconscious, I pivoted away, and when I took my first step toward the door, Stevenson groaned. I turned to him. His eyes flickered open as whispers flowed from his moving lips. I stepped to his bedside and arched toward him.

He inhaled a labored breath before exhaling and mumbling, "Fi—find her. Mancini."

"Mancini?" I repeated.

Stevenson sighed, then closed his eyes, his breathing slowly regulating. I figured he was still on pain meds and wasn't all coherent, so I left the room. *Who's Mancini?* I thought on the elevator ride down. As I passed through the lobby, I saw Hiller talking to the nurse at the receptionist's counter. He didn't notice me, so I continued to the parking garage where I passed two more uniform officers on the way to my car.

I had a little under eleven hours left and no leads. While inside my car, I dialed Keith, figuring it would be a good idea to get my payment sooner rather than later and deposit it, just in case I ended up in jail before the end of the day.

"What's up, cuz?" Keith answered.

"Are you able to meet me sooner?" I asked.

"Yeah—yeah, when?"

"Twenty minutes."

"Cool. Same place?"

"Yep."

Seventeen minutes later, I pulled into the parking lot near The Florida Aquarium like I did the day before. To my surprise, Keith parked a few spaces from me a moment later. I left my gun in the glove compartment and exited the car.

I walked to Keith's car. "You're actually on time," I said to him as he stepped out from behind the wheel.

Keith shrugged. "I was in the neighborhood," he said before closing the car door. "It's back here."

I followed him to the trunk. While he opened it and leaned inside, I surveyed the area. A moment later, he emerged with a brown paper bag in hand.

"A paper bag?" I said as he handed it to me.

"Man, that's all I had at the time," Keith said before smiling and shutting the trunk. "But it's twenty stacks."

Inside the bag were two stacks of one hundred-dollar bills. Both stacks were separately banded with a paper bill strap indicating ten thousand was in each. I examined a few bills and immediately knew they were real. A skill I picked up during my time on the force and honed in my current line of work.

I placed the bag under my armpit. "Looks good," I said while pivoting toward my car.

Keith clapped his hands together. "Alright," he said, following me to the Caddy.

I popped my trunk and settled the bag in a hidden compartment off to the side.

"You gonna be able to get that condo in no time," Keith said.

I shut the trunk. "And whatchu gonna do with your portion?" I asked him.

"There's some other—investments I'm looking to make."

I shook my head. "Betta be legal and stable investments."

As I uttered those words, a familiar, 2012 Chevy Caprice cruised along the road on the opposite side of the parking lot. The vehicle was a pearl black with silver trimming and tinted windows.

"Were you followed?" I asked Keith.

Keith winced and said, "Nah, man," before following my gaze to the Caprice. "Wait. That's Terrell's car."

"I thought so."

"Chance, we gotta bounce."

"He's not stupid enough to try sumpin' in a public area."

The Caprice whipped into the parking lot and sped toward us.

"Maybe I'm wrong," I said. "Split up!"

Keith ran in the aquarium's direction while I darted toward the park. The car screeched to a stop. Terrell, the skinny guy with the nappy hair, and the bald man all emerged from the car. Terrell pointed toward me and yelled, "Get 'em," before rushing after Keith.

Nappy and the Baldy hustled in my direction. I bolted into the park and ran the paved pathway for fifty meters before veering across an open field and through a small, wooded area. I glanced over my shoulder and saw Nappy and Baldy hurrying across the field. Once out of the woods, I ran toward the public restrooms and hid behind the small building. I reached behind my back and felt disappointed when I realized I had left my gun in the car. *Guess Imma have to do this the old fashion way,* I thought.

As I peeked around the corner, I saw the men exit the woods. They stopped running and scanned the area with their heads on a swivel. The restroom building was the only standing structure close by, so they immediately turned their attention to it. I weaved my head behind the corner, then rested my back against the wall and listened. Footsteps and heavy panting breaths approached. I peeked around the corner and saw the two men near the front of the restrooms. Nappy held a pistol. Baldy's hands were empty.

"You think he went inside?" Baldy asked.

"I don't know," Nappy said. "Go see while I check the back."

He circled the building on my side. I eased behind the corner and waited. Nappy's footsteps crunched over leaves and twigs as he made his way closer to me. As his gun's barrel inched around the corner, I clenched it, then twisted my wrist as if I was turning a doorknob. The skinny man yelped as I yanked him toward me and delivered a devastating cross to his jaw.

Nappy went to sleep as he leaned to the side and fell to the ground. With the gun aimed, I eased along the wall toward the front of the building. As I turned the corner, the Baldy exited the women's restroom. He winced, then charged at me, ramming into me as I struggled to bring the gun to bear. The firearm flung from my hands and scraped across the pavement. I shoved him, then shuffled backward off the pavement onto the ground. He launched toward me with a wild punch. Bobbing under his attack, I struck his exposed ribcage with a right hook, then a left. Baldy immediately hugged his midsection and sunk toward the ground. With his face wide open, I connected a crushing cross to his jaw. His eyes closed, and he fell to the leaves and dirt.

"Weak chins," I uttered to myself, picking up the gun and jogging back into the woods.

I hustled through the park, back toward the aquarium, and in the direction I last saw Terrell chase after Keith. The track led me along the side of the aquarium and to the back, where a small plot of grass and a view of the Ybor Channel's still waters greeted me. With my head on a swivel, I surveyed the area and noticed a shabby deck leading to an old boat shed. As I made my way toward the shed, I heard voices flow from inside. I raced across the creaky dock and yanked the shed's door open in time to hear Terrell yell, "Ya'll think ya'll can punk me—" He had his gun trained on Keith, but as the door slammed behind me, he swung the pistol in my direction. While he pivoted toward me, I grabbed his firearm with my free hand, then pistol-slapped him with the gun in my other hand. Terrell stumbled toward the back of the shed. Keith dodged around the staggering man and circled to the door.

I pointed both guns at Terrell. "I thought I told you not to mess with me or my family," I said.

He stepped back with his chin raised and nose crinkled. "You tough with those guns, huh?" he said before shaking his head. "I ain't scared of you."

I cocked my head to the side, squinted at him, then looked at the guns. "You think I need these?" I said, a slight chuckle in my voice.

Terrell shrugged. I shook my head and walked toward a window at the shed's sidewall. Once there, I tossed the guns through the broken glass. The pistols splashed as they hit the water.

"You hafta be running low on guns," I said, walking back to Terrell. "That's three I've taken from you in less than forty-eight hours."

Terrell grimaced.

I shrugged. "No guns. Now what?"

Terrell nodded and raised his fists. "Okay."

He threw a jab. I weaved from the attack's path. Terrell followed up with a cross. I bobbed under the punch and struck him in the gut. He shuffled backward and doubled over.

"Done already?" I taunted him.

Terrell looked at me with gritted teeth. From his pocket, he removed a knife and flicked it open. Growling, he charged toward me with the blade drawn back above his shoulder. I stepped forward, hit his nose with a quick jab, then grabbed his knife-wielding arm and used his momentum to toss him over my hip and to the floor. Air huffed from his mouth as his back hit and splintered the wood beneath him.

"Whoa," Keith enthused.

With Terrell's arm still in my grip, I locked his elbow and took possession of the blade. As the thug lay sprawled on the floor, I closed the knife and placed it inside my pocket, then patted him down for any other weapons. I felt something jingle in his left pants pocket. I removed the item, and my mouth fell open when I recognized it.

In my hand rested the same gold bracelet I saw Eve wearing the other night. It had the same heart-shaped diamonds. I was sure of it.

"Where did you get this?" I asked Terrell.

He leaned forward and coughed. "Nonna yo business," he said.

I kneeled and grabbed his collar. "You betta start talking," I said.

Terrell smirked.

I yanked his collar until he was a few inches off the floor, then slammed him back to the floor. Terrell gasped.

"Where'd you get it?" I said, wagging the bracelet in front of him.

He coughed. "From some chick. What's it to you?"

"What she look like?"

"I don't know. Curly hair. Plump lips. Plump butt. She was bad. Didn't wanna give me her number, so I made her give me the bracelet."

"Where was this?"

"You asking a lot of questions."

I yanked Terrell by his collar again.

"Wait, wait," he protested. "Near Riverview. Across the street from the mall—by the water where those new townhomes are."

"I know the place. Was she staying there?"

"I don't know. It was getting dark. Didn't see where she came from, but looked like she was heading toward the townhomes."

"You betta not be lying."

"I'm not."

I released Terrell's collar. "And when I say stay away from me and my family, I mean it," I told him before jabbing his face.

Terrell's head hit the floor, and he immediately took a nap. I stood and settled the bracelet in my pocket, then headed straight for the door.

"What's goin' on?" Keith asked, trailing behind me as we crossed the deck.

"I'll explain later. Let's get outta here."

When we made it back to the parking lot, I removed Terrell's knife and poked a hole in both back tires of his Caprice.

"That's gonna make him mad," Keith said.

"So?" I said.

Keith shook his head.

"Why don't you hang low for a couple of days?" I continued. "You know—stay outta sight."

Keith shrugged. "Okay."

I slid behind the wheel of the Caddy and started the engine. Keith entered his car and followed me onto the main street. I turned right, and he turned left. After driving a quarter of a mile, I dialed my cop buddy.

"McCoach," he answered.

"Hey, it's me," I said.

"Tell me you have something. You have nine and a half hours."

"Plenty of time. I may have something, but not sure."

"Tell me what it is."

I shook my head at the phone. "I will once I follow up on it. Want to confirm before I have you chasing down a dead lead."

"Okay then."

"But there is a suspicious group at the aquarium. They're driving a black Caprice. You may wanna check it out."

"Should I even ask?"

"Probably not."

McCoach chuckled. "I'll have a unit sent."

"Thanks. Hey, does the name Mancini mean anything to you?"

"Mancini, Mancini. The only Mancini I know are mobsters."

"The mob?"

"Yeah. They're big in New York City. An old friend of mine at the New York District Attorney's office has been working for years to shut them down. Why?"

"Stevenson mentioned the name. May be a good idea to put a security detail on him."

"I already did. Sent a unit this morning."

"Hiller?" I asked.

"No, a couple of uniforms. What are you thinking?"

"Not sure. But I'll let you know as soon as I figure it out."

"I'll be waiting."

I ended the call and headed for the Riverview Mall. On the way, I dialed Darla to have her look into any connections between the Stevensons and Mancinis. The mall's parking lot was sparse, so it was easy to find a spot facing the townhomes across the street. I had an unobstructed view of the community's entrance. The small neighborhood comprised of fifteen or twenty new waterfront units, with a few more under construction. Most looked empty, and the community was quiet with little activity. Not much vehicle traffic moved on the main road near the entrance, and very little foot traffic used the sidewalks. I looked down the street and saw a few old, dilapidated buildings maybe two blocks away.

Gentrification. I cracked the car windows, adjusted in my seat, and waited.

An hour passed when I looked in my rearview mirror and noticed a familiar figure leaving the mall. As the silhouette came closer, I knew without a doubt it was Eve. She wore a fitted white blouse and dark jeans. With a bag in her hand, she crossed the street and walked toward the townhome community. I grabbed my pistol and exited the car. Quickly stuffing the gun in my back waistband, I darted across the street and followed Eve onto the sidewalk at a distance. I increased my pace until we were only twenty feet away from each other.

She stopped walking. I ducked behind a unit and peeked around the corner. Eve surveyed her surroundings before continuing up the sidewalk. I followed. She walked to a home near the end of the community and removed a key. I made note of the house number, and when she unlocked the door, I rushed to her.

"Get in," I said, forcing her inside and shutting the door.

"Hey, wait," she protested.

"Hi, Eve," I said as we stood in a partially furnished living room.

A couch, a television, and a shelf with a few trophies occupied the space. One thing that really caught my attention was a poster with a stick and knife crossing. Eskrima was written at the top of the poster.

Eve's mouth fell open. "Chance? What—what are you doing here?" She spoke as if she was out of breath.

I circled her. "I could ask you the same thing. There's a lot of people looking for you, Eve."

Her eyes widened as footsteps approached behind me. "No, wait!" she said.

Before I could turn, something hard struck the back of my head, then blackness veiled my eyes.

12

As I opened my eyes, I realized I was on a carpeted floor in a room with one door and one window. I had a pounding headache. My hands were bound together. So were my legs. Both with cotton rope. Small slits of light squeezed through the closed window blinds and provided faint illumination to the empty room. I adjusted myself so my back sat against the wall. Voices flowed from the opposite side of the door. One voice I recognized as Eve's. She was arguing with a man.

A moment later, the room's door opened, and she stepped inside. As we stared at each other, I noticed the energy drain from her face. Like she was concerned or worried.

"Don't look at me like that," I said.

She took two steps toward me. "Are you okay?" she asked.

"You and your boyfriend knocked me out, then tied me up. Whatchu think?"

"I'm sorry." She walked to me and kneeled. "I tried to stop it."

I rolled my eyes and looked away. "Yeah."

"What are you doing here, Chance?"

"Looking for you."

Eve winced. "Why?"

"Your husband hired me to find you."

"What? No, he hired some investigator in St. Pete to find me."

Before I could respond, the room's door swung open. A familiar-looking man with an athletic built stood at the door. His bruised left jaw and black right eye sat prominently on his light-brown face.

The man placed a hand on top of his curly hair and slid his hand to his forehead. "That's what I've been tryna tell you," he said to Eve. "He's the guy from that PI's office."

"You mean the man you killed?" I taunted him.

He pointed at me. "Watch ya mouth. I didn't kill him. He was dead when I got there."

"Calm down, Will," Eve told the man.

"Will," I said before looking at Eve. "Is he your boyfriend? He looks like Patrick." I glanced at Will. "Yeah, you definitely have a type."

Will stepped into the room. "Keep talking and I'll cut ya tongue out."

"Sure, whateva."

"You think I'm playin' with you?"

Eve stood and walked to Will with her palms aimed at him. "Look. I need a word with him," she said.

"You betta tell him to watch his mouth."

"William!"

Will looked at Eve.

"Please give me a moment."

Will glanced at me, then Eve, before nodding and leaving the room.

"That boy's a piece of work," I said to Eve's back. "Just like your husband. You sure know how to pick'em. Was your father around when you were a little girl?"

She turned to me. "Chance. I need to know everything Patrick told you."

I shrugged. "He didn't tell me much. Said to just locate you."

"That's it? Anything else?"

"Oh. He also said you were cheating on him."

"This isn't funny, Chance. Someone came after me."

"At your motel?" I asked.

Eve's eyebrows furrowed.

"Why were you at a motel anyway when your boyfriend has a townhome?"

She glanced at the floor.

"Oh, I see. You were hiding something from Will. Or maybe you were planning on breaking up with him. Was that why you were at the bar? Looking for the next sucka?"

Eve jolted her head. "Y—you don't understand."

"I understand there's a dead private investigator and your husband is laid up in the hospital."

"What?" Eve said. Legitimate concern filled her eyes.

"You didn't hear? Some accident. Hit-and-run."

Eve paced the floor. "Okay, okay, okay," she mumbled before facing me. "You need to tell me everything you know."

"I did."

She shook her head. "No, you know more," she said while pointing at me.

"Sorry, babe. You know more than I do now. Tell me, why does he want to find you so bad?"

Eve pivoted toward the door. "I'll give you some time to think about it," she said with her back to me. "Then I'll send

Will in. He knows martial arts. Good with knives. If you talk, he may untie you."

"Is that some kinda threat?"

Still with her back to me, she sighed. "It's not meant to be. I'll be back."

I shook my head as she left the room, and the door shut. Will may be good with a knife, but he lacked experience in this game. My keys, wallet, Eve's bracelet, and Terrell's knife were still in my pockets. Only my pistol was missing. Removing the knife from my pocket posed a bit of a challenge, mainly because my hands were big. Flipping it open was even more challenging, but positioning the blade at a part of the rope that wouldn't cut my hand was the most tricky part.

As I sawed the rope, I heard faint chatter from the room opposite the door. The voices fell silent and two brisk knocks flowed from the townhome's front door. Someone said something, but I found it difficult to make out what was being said. Footsteps rapidly approached the room. I dropped the knife to the floor and concealed it with my thigh. The door swung open, and Eve entered. Her eyes were wide, and concern stretched across her face.

She put a finger to her lips. "You need to be quiet," she said.

"First you want me to talk, now I hafta be quiet?" I said.

She exhaled and shook her head before grabbing a long, drape-looking cloth from the floor and tying it around my mouth, gagging me.

"Stay quiet," she said before leaving and closing the door.

I picked up the knife and continued cutting.

I was halfway through the rope when I heard more talking from the other room. Suddenly, a boisterous crash flowed from the door. Eve screamed. Shouting and stomps followed. I finished cutting through the rope, then quickly removed the gag and untied my legs. As I unwound the loose strands from my ankles, the roar of two gunshots smacked against the room's door. Eve's screams grew louder, then abruptly stopped. I zipped to the door and nudged it open. Peeking through the slit, I saw Will sprawled on the floor. A male figure dressed in dark clothing threw Eve over his shoulder and walked toward the front door. When the door closed behind them, I rushed to Will. Two bullet holes in his chest oozed blood.

"Ahh," he gurgled as a red bubble formed in his mouth and then popped.

I kneeled over him.

"A cop," he said before taking a final breath and closing his eyes.

My gun lay on the floor next to him. I inspected it. He hadn't fired it. Outside, a vehicle door thumped closed. I hurried to the door, and as my eyes adjusted to the light, a silver SUV with a dented front bumper, shattered headlight, and busted grill jetted past, stringing a trail of smoke behind it. I hustled through the community toward the main street. The SUV exited the community, bolting by as I crossed the street. When I reached my car, I brought the Caddy's engine to life and sped from the parking lot after the SUV. The vehicle was maybe thirty yards from me. It made a left at an intersection. I was sure I wouldn't catch it when the traffic ahead of me halted for a red light. I slammed the brakes and the car jerked to a stop. Gripping the steering wheel, I exhaled. After a minute, traffic eased forward, and I removed my phone. Ignoring the missed calls, I dialed McCoach.

"A little over eight hours left," he answered.

"Yeah, I'm not worried about that. I found her."

"Okay. Where is she?"

"With her kidnapper."

"What?"

"Someone took her. Killed her lover in the process."

"Where?" McCoach asked.

I gave him the location and number for the townhome.

"I tracked her there, and they got the drop on me. Shortly after I woke, someone entered the house, killed the boyfriend and took her."

"I'll send a couple of red and blues there. Where are you now?"

"Was in pursuit of the vehicle but lost them."

"Did you get the tag?"

"I didn't. They were moving too fast and trailing smoke."

"What kinda car was it?"

"Silver SUV. May have been an Explorer."

"Sounds like the vehicle that fled Stevenson's accident."

"Now that's interesting," I said.

"Thanks to CCTV footage, we got a number from the plate. The SUV belongs to a Benjamin Greer."

"So, he's your guy?"

"Well, he's the primary suspect for the hit-and-run, and now looks like we can add kidnapping."

"And murder."

"Yeah. And murder. Hiller went to Greer's home address. Should hear from him shortly—actually, I'll probably call him after I get off with you."

"What's the address?"

"If I tell you, am I gonna regret it?" McCoach said.

"My man, there's a lot about this you already regret. Just add it to my tab."

13

Fifteen minutes later, I turned onto a street heading toward Benjamin Greer's home. It was in a quiet neighborhood on the east side of Brandon. Large oak trees and stucco ranch-style homes with manicured yards rolled by as I cruised the freshly paved road. After driving a couple hundred yards, the road became bumpy and the yards unkempt. I eased down the street for another minute before seeing the number I was looking for. It was on a mailbox near the end of the street. The front yard was spacious, but untidy, littered with car parts, boxes, and a variety of other mechanical scraps. An older bungalow style home sat in the yard. The house had a screened porch and dirty tan vinyl siding with faded black trimming.

I parked by an empty field a little ways from the house. McCoach had told me not to do anything. Said to sit tight and wait for the cops. But since I didn't work for him, I took it as a suggestion. I grabbed my gun, then emerged from the Caddy and into the cool shade. Holding the gun to my side, I crept toward the house while surveying the area. I entered the yard and threaded around a rusted nineteen eight-six Pontiac Firebird frame on blocks.

Footsteps crunching over twigs and leaves flowed from the back. With my gun trained, I crept along the side of the house. On my way to the back, I noticed a defined vehicular path on the ground and a shabby car shed in the backyard. More footsteps from the back crushed the sticks and foliage beneath it. When I turned the corner, an athletic man in dark slacks and a polo shirt stood in front of me with his arms raised.

"Don't move," I said.

We stared at one another for a few seconds until we registered each other's face.

"Hiller," I said.

"Yeah. You're McCoach's friend, right?"

"Right," I said, slowly lowering my gun.

Hiller touched his chest. "You scared me," he said while using his free hand to rake his messy, dirty blond hair backward.

"We tracked a suspect to this address," Hiller said, nearly out of breath. "Doesn't appear anyone's here, though."

I nodded. "Okay," I said, walking closer to the house to inspect the back door.

It looked closed.

Panting, Hiller hunched over and touched his knees.

"You okay?" I asked.

"Yeah. I ran around the house earlier. Thought I heard footsteps, but it was a stray cat. Then you scared me and took what breath I had left."

My phone rang. I took a few steps away from the house and Hiller before removing it from my pocket.

"Yep," I answered.

"Did you not get my missed calls?" Darla said.

"Sorry, but a woman had me tied up."

"Hilarious. Listen, I looked into Stevenson and the Mancinis. And my hunch was right."

"Okay," I said into the phone while glancing at Hiller as he waved for my attention.

"Imma call this in," he mouthed before turning and heading to the side of the house.

"Seems many of those LLCs Stevenson owns are shell companies," Darla continued. "Victor Mancini is a member with him on several companies, so he has to be laundering Mancini's money."

"Okay, so Stevenson's dirty. That's no surprise. What does this have to do with Eve?"

"Hello, she's married to Stevenson. Maybe a deal with Mancini went sideways."

"Then why not just go directly after Stevenson?"

"The Mancinis are mobsters. Maybe they want to make an example."

"I get that, but there's more. Why go through all this trouble for an example?"

"It's no trouble for them," Darla said. "These people have connections all throughout the judicial system."

"I'm sure they're pretty connected."

"They are. It's nothing for them to have cops or maybe even judges in their pocket. Some months back, Stevenson and Victor Mancini were persons of interest in an NYPD Internal Affairs investigation involving a cop. Apparently, the detective was caught with a large bag of cash. The bag had one of Stevenson's and Mancini's companies' logo on it."

"Really?"

"Yep. It's amazing what you find when you dig deep enough."

"What happened to the cop?"

"You know how it goes. Suspended for a little while, then back to work."

"Who was the cop?" I asked, turning toward the car shed. *I didn't see his car!*

Out of pure instinct, I ducked.

"Greg Hiller," Darla's faint voice said as the phone dropped from my hand and a loud blast erupted behind me.

14

I dove to the ground while a cocktail of sounds flooded my ears. Darla calling to me through the phone, a bullet whizzing past my shoulder, and the thunderous echo from a gunshot. While falling toward the dirt and leaves, I spun and saw Hiller in a weaver stance with his pistol pointed in my direction—the white of his eyes exposed and his teeth gritted. His aim followed my descent, but I already had my gun trained on him. I fired a round before landing on the ground. A deafening roar swept across the yard as a bullet penetrated Hiller's shoulder, causing him to drop his gun.

I thrust myself from the ground and into a kneeling position to prepare for another shot. Hiller rushed me before I could bring my gun to bear. He grabbed me in a tackle and my gun flew from my hand as we both toppled to the ground. We rolled in the grass, grabbing and clawing. It ended with Hiller straddling me. He threw a punch. I parried his attack, then jabbed him in the nose before hooking the back of his head and slinging him to the ground. I rolled onto my belly and pushed myself up. Hiller did the same. As we stood, he wiped his nose with his sleeve.

"So, you're the Mancini's lapdog?" I said.

Hiller just gritted his teeth.

"You killed Finley and put Stevenson in the hospital."

Hiller smirked. "Yeah, I did. And after I kill you—I'm gonna take care of that woman, then finish what I started with Stevenson."

"So, she's still alive?"

"Don't worry about it," Hiller said, raising his fists. "You won't be alive long enough for it to matter."

I raised my fists, and we squared off. Hiller jabbed with a right. I weaved out of the attack's path. He followed up with a left jab, and I weaved to the opposite side before landing a jab on his forehead and following up with a cross to his jaw. He staggered backward.

I shook my head. "You won't beat me in a fistfight, my man. Especially with that injured shoulder. Stop this and turn yourself in."

Hiller growled and blitzed toward me. He grabbed me in a tackle and rammed my back against an oak tree.

He struck my right ribcage with a hook, then my left. I mushed his face. His head snapped back, and his body followed as he stumbled backward. I rubbed my elbows against my sides to soothe the stinging.

"How that feel?" Hiller taunted.

I set my chin and raised my fist. Hiller launched at me and threw a nearly perfect cross. He had his feet planted, his form was good, but he misjudged the distance between us and overextended his attack. I leaned back. The punch breezed past an inch away from my face. I slipped to Hiller's outside and delivered a devastating hook to his ribcage. As he shrunk under the pain, I followed up with another hook to his stomach.

Hiller hugged his lower body, leaving his upper body completely exposed. I hit his chin with a left cross, then his jaw with a right. Hiller flopped to the ground. He moaned as he rolled to his hands and knees. He whipped his head to the right. I followed his gaze and saw his gun. Hiller crawled toward the pistol. I scanned the ground and spotted my gun slightly burrowed under sticks and leaves. I ran and slid to the ground after my weapon. Grabbing the gun, I turned to Hiller. He spun toward me with his gun in hand. I aimed at him and pulled the trigger twice. The first round hit his chest and the second near his neck. Hiller dropped his gun, gasped, then fell backward and sprawled on the grass.

Wincing at the various aches shooting throughout my body, I stood and walked to Hiller. I kicked his gun away from him and kneeled to frisk him. I didn't find any other weapons or his pulse. Standing, I stuffed my gun in my back waistband, then scanned the ground for my phone. When I picked it up, Darla screamed my name.

"Okay, I'm here," I said into the phone

"Are you okay? What was that noise?" she asked.

"Death knocking on the door, but it wasn't for me."

"I'm calling the cops."

"No need. They're on the way."

"You sure?"

"Positive. I have to go. And thanks, baby doll. You saved my life."

"Oh my goodness, be careful."

"Aren't I always?"

I ended the call and surveyed the yard. My attention quickly went to the car shed. As I approached the shed, the faint sound of engines turning over and car doors shutting flowed from behind the structure. Looking behind the shed, I saw the parking lot of a popular department store past a wooded area in the distance. I returned to the front of the car shed and lifted the door. It rolled open and the scent of death struck my nose. Inside, the busted silver SUV stood parked front and center. In the back corner, a man sat on the floor, leaning against the wall. Swatting flies away, I hurried to him. While inspecting him for a pulse, I found a thin laceration circling his neck but no pulse.

Benjamin Greer, I figured.

Standing from the body, I noticed the SUV's trunk ajar. I raised the door a few inches before the hydraulics took over and opened the door completely. A black jacket and duffel bag sat on the floor. I unzipped the bag and stacks of one hundred-dollar bills fell from the bag. Before I could fully process what happened, the vehicle shook, and a muffled moan flowed from the back seat.

I circled to the passenger's side back door. When I opened the door, Eve lay in the seat with her hands duct-taped behind her. Her ankles were also tied together, and a strip of tape stretched across her mouth. I pulled the tape from her mouth.

"Chance!" she said. "You have to help me. He's—"

I stuck the tape back around her mouth. She didn't groan or fight, but her furrowed eyebrows said everything. With the knife from my pocket, I cut the tape from around her ankles and helped her out of the vehicle. I guided her outside the shed and sat her on the grass. I removed the tape from her mouth once more.

"You gonna untie my hands from behind me?"

I pressed the tape back on. She protested briefly before staring at me. Her eyes asked questions I didn't care to answer. I walked back inside the shed and grabbed the duffel bag from the SUV, then stepped outside and tossed the bag at her feet.

I removed the tape once again. "Now you may talk," I said before pointing at the bag. "Start with telling me about this."

Eve looked at the ground and sighed.

"Today, hon!" I said.

She looked at me. "I took it."

I nodded as if to say, no kidding.

"As you already know," she continued, "Patrick and I have had issues for a while."

"Issues? Meaning you cheated?"

"He cheated long before I stepped out on him. He's not the clean businessman he presents himself to be. Been stealing from the Mancinis long before I took this money."

I squinted.

"Oh, you didn't know? Patrick's been siphoning the Mancinis' money to offshore accounts for years. He did it in small amounts, so it didn't immediately raise any flags. He must've thought I was too stupid to understand the paperwork, because he knew I had access to the safe where he kept the documents." Eve chuckled. "I guess he forgot I majored in finance."

"You knew the money belonged to the Mancinis and took it anyway?"

Eve shrugged. "I needed to get away from Patrick for a fresh start. So, when I saw the bag in his office, I took it."

"This was three weeks ago?"

"Yeah, I guess so."

"How did Hiller end up with the money?"

"Hiller?"

"The guy that kidnapped you."

"He had to be the one who took it from my motel room.

Took my cellphone too. At first, I thought the private investigator Patrick hired a while back had something to do with it."

"That's why you sent your boyfriend to his office. You thought he had the money."

Eve glanced at the ground, then back at me before nodding. "Yeah. But when Will got there, he found the man dead. Said he was shot. But I promise you, Chance, I didn't hurt anyone or mean for anyone to get hurt."

"That may be true, doll, but your boyfriend's dead and your husband's in the hospital."

Eve sighed. "Patrick," she said, shaking her head. "How'd we get here?"

"Easy. The Mancinis found about his scheme and wanted him dead." I shrugged. "I'm guessing they've known for a while. And with you being his wife, they may have thought you were involved, so when you took the money, they probably saw it as a play and decided to kill you two. I'm sure they've been keeping tabs on you for some time. You were never gonna get away and start fresh."

Sirens wailed in the distance.

Eve looked in that direction. "You used to be a cop. How bad does it look, Chance?" she asked.

I removed her bracelet from my pocket and walked to her. Kneeling, I placed it in her pocket, then stood. She stared at me like she wanted to ask a question but said nothing.

"Four people are dead, sweetheart. Doesn't look good," I told her.

She hung her head.

"Why did you come to the jazz club?"

She hunched her shoulders before looking at me, her eyes misty. "I just wanted to get away from it for a while."

"Running away from your double life. That's something."

"I didn't mean for you to get involved."

I believed her. "I'm sure you didn't, hon," I said. "But you were scheming, just like Patrick."

Eve nodded. "I was."

"But I think you're gonna be alright." I grinned. "Just remember to practice what you preach, though," I said, eliciting a forced smile from her.

My phone rang. I stepped away and answered it.

"Chance!" McCoach answered.

"What's up?"

"I had suspicions about Hiller's investigation, so I looked into him and found—"

"I know," I interrupted. "I'll see you when you get here," I told him before ending the call.

15

An hour later, the sun began its descent. I sat on the rear bumper of an ambulance parked in the middle of Greer's front yard with my eyes fixed on the gorgeous, slender, female paramedic disinfecting my cuts and bruises. She noticed me looking. I smiled. She smiled back.

"What?" she asked in a playful tone, her short, dark feathered hair bouncing as her chin dropped and her penetrating hazel eyes locked with mine.

I shrugged my mouth. "I was just wondering."

"Wondering what?" she asked, gently pressing a small bandage over a cut on my cheek.

"What time you get off?"

She cocked her head to the side and looked at me while removing her latex gloves and smiling. "We're finished," she said.

"No, not already."

"Yes, I'm sorry."

McCoach approached the ambulance. The paramedic turned to him.

"He checks out," she told McCoach before glancing back

at me. "But I'll have to keep an eye on him," she continued before disappearing toward the front of the ambulance.

"You still haven't learned your lesson," McCoach said.

I shrugged.

"You were right," McCoach continued. "The body in the shed is Greer. We found Hiller's car parked at the department store on the other side of the woods. The working theory is he parked there and came over here to steal Greer's SUV."

"Greer has a record?"

"Yep. Robbery and attempted murder."

I nodded. "Makes sense. Hiller probably thought he'd make a good scapegoat."

"Right. But Hiller didn't get a chance to stage it." McCoach sighed. "With him dead, that makes four bodies."

"Could've been more."

"What makes you say that?"

"Myself and Eve. And then Stevenson, if you didn't send that security detail to the hospital."

"Maybe Stevenson and Eve. But I don't see you going down easily."

"Ain't that the truth," I said before staring at McCoach. "You know, I feel bad for Jacob Finley's family. He was just doing his job. And when he realized how deep it went, he handed the matter over to the authorities but still ended up dead."

"Is that your way of explaining why you didn't let the authorities know sooner? Your justification?"

I stood. "Like I mentioned, there was a crook in the department. If I had gone to Tampa PD too soon with this, I could've been the fifth dead body."

"I had my suspicions about Hiller but never investigated his past. You were a cop, so you know how it is. We want to assume the best of our fellow brothers." McCoach shook his head. "An oversight on my part."

"I wouldn't sweat that too much. The Mancinis probably have people around the country."

"Well, I plan to contact my district attorney friend in New York. With the Stevensons' testimony, I believe the DA's office can build a strong case against the Mancinis."

"What makes you think they'll testify?" I asked.

"When they see the charges we stack against them, they'll be ready to cut a deal."

I hunched my shoulders and nodded. "Smart play. Just know I won't be testifying."

McCoach sighed. "I can't make any promises," he said.

"I can."

McCoach shook his head. "Either way. I need you to come down to the station tomorrow. Still a lot more to sort out."

"I know the drill," I said, pivoting away from him and heading in my car's direction. "I'll be there right after I go to the hospital."

"You betta not be going to intimidate Stevenson into testifying. I want the pleasure of doing that."

I stopped walking and turned to McCoach. "The only thing I want from Stevenson and this entire situation is the rest of my money."

McCoach chuckled, then disappeared into the busyness of the crime scene, and I threaded around a few squad cars on the way to the Caddy. As I settled behind the wheel, an officer escorting Eve to a cruiser caught my eye. I watched as Eve paced to the vehicle in what seemed like slow-motion strides—her eyes bulging and watery, her mouth gaped. I couldn't believe she was the same woman I saw two nights prior.

I called Darla to let her know I was okay and to work the rest of the week from home. She offered to patch my wounds, but I informed her that a sweet young paramedic beat her to it.

"You haven't learned, have you?" she asked before abruptly ending the call.

I started the car and headed for the jazz club.

The band started their first set as I entered and ambled to my usual seat at the bar. Robby emerged from the kitchen. He stopped in front of the doors and winced.

"What happened to you?" he asked.

I cocked my head. "Just one of those days," I said.

"Right." Robby chuckled and leaned over the bar top toward me. "It has nothing to do with that woman?"

I shrugged. "How 'bout you cut me a break tonight?"

Robby chuckled. "Alright, alright," he said with his hands raised in a surrendered posture.

"Thank you."

Robby again leaned over the bar top. "So, did you at least get to the bottom of it?"

"Don't I always?"

Robby stood. "I guess. You wantcha usual?"

"Yeah, that sounds good."

"Coming right up, my brutha."

Robby poured me a club soda with grapefruit juice, then waved to someone across the room before disappearing into the kitchen. I sat with my drink and enjoyed the music while the band finished their set. The audience immediately clapped and cheered. Slowly, the hoots and applauses died down, and the club's front door opened. A tall, fit woman wearing a black bodycon dress entered. She had hazelnut skin and a short bob cut. A shorter woman with longer hair walked in behind her. The tall woman exchanged some words with her friend before glancing at me. I looked away, keeping my eyes on my drink as the two women made their way to the bar. They sat one stool away with the tall woman closest to me.

As they chit chatted, I kept my sights ahead and sipped my drink. Maybe McCoach and Darla were wrong. Maybe I had learned my lesson. After a few moments, the short woman stood and walked toward the bathrooms. In my peripheral, I saw the tall woman flick her hair, then glance at me. I fought to not look at her but couldn't resist. Felt like a motor was torquing my head in her direction. We locked eyes and she smiled. I smiled back.

Maybe I haven't learned my lesson.

THANK YOU FOR READING

I have a favor to ask. If you have a moment, I would really appreciate it if you could leave a short review on the page where you purchased this book. I'm thankful for you sharing your feedback about this book. It really helps new readers find this series.

Sign up for notifications of new books by Alex Cage and exclusive giveaways

www.AlexCage.com/signup

MORE BY ALEX CAGE

More books by Alex Cage. Have you read them all? Grab your next adventure today!

Orlando Black Series

Carolina Dance

Bayside Boom

Bet on Black

Leroy Silver Series

Contracts & Bullets

Aloha & Bullets

Politics Thieves & Bullets

Get the latest releases and exclusive giveaways, sign up to the Alex Cage Reader List.

www.AlexCage.com/signup

ABOUT THE AUTHOR

Alex Cage is a thriller author and passionate wordsmith who loves to blend his fascination with martial arts and travel with high-octane action and explosive adventures. He enjoys nothing more than entertaining his readers with death-defying missions, larger-than-life characters, and suspenseful stories that always find a way to keep you on your toes.

As the author of nearly a dozen titles, including the Orlando Black series and the Leroy Silver series, Alex combines his obsession for thrillers with a sprinkling of fantasy and sci-fi, so that readers will always find something to capture their imagination. He currently resides in North Carolina. When not writing his next novel, you can find him reading and practicing martial arts.

Find out more about Alex Cage (and get a free read):

www.alexcage.com
connect@alexcage.com

ALEX CAGE
CLEAN FAST-PACED ACTION THRILLERS